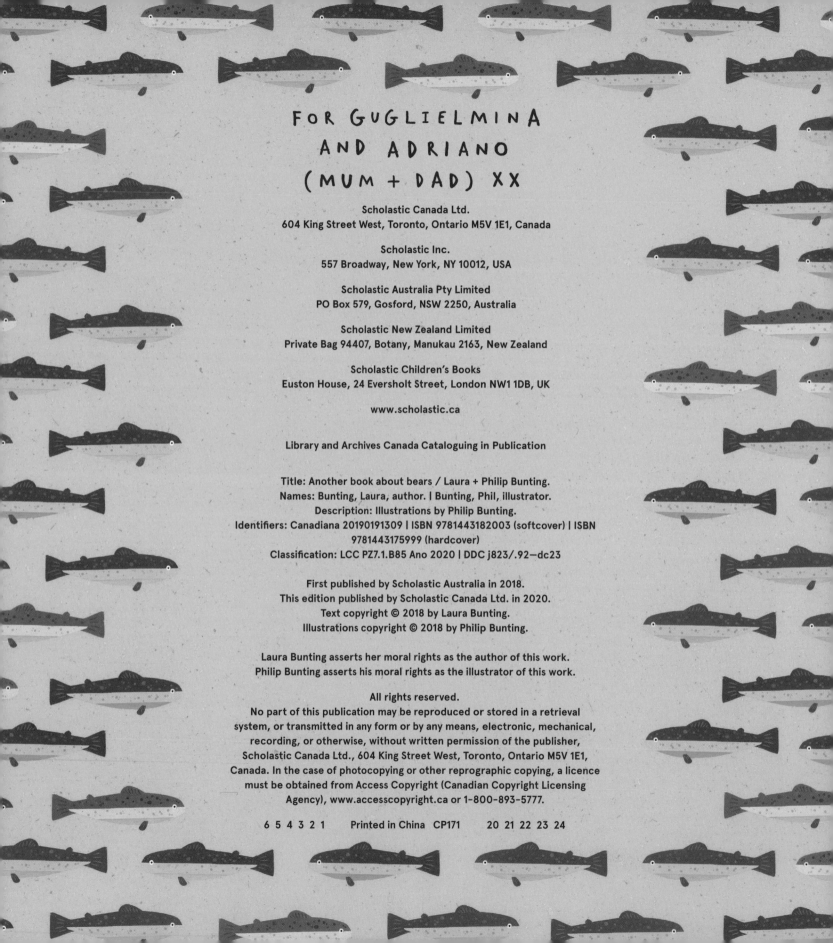

FOR GUGLIELMINA
AND ADRIANO
(MUM + DAD) XX

Scholastic Canada Ltd.
604 King Street West, Toronto, Ontario M5V 1E1, Canada

Scholastic Inc.
557 Broadway, New York, NY 10012, USA

Scholastic Australia Pty Limited
PO Box 579, Gosford, NSW 2250, Australia

Scholastic New Zealand Limited
Private Bag 94407, Botany, Manukau 2163, New Zealand

Scholastic Children's Books
Euston House, 24 Eversholt Street, London NW1 1DB, UK

www.scholastic.ca

Library and Archives Canada Cataloguing in Publication

Title: Another book about bears / Laura + Philip Bunting.
Names: Bunting, Laura, author. | Bunting, Phil, illustrator.
Description: Illustrations by Philip Bunting.
Identifiers: Canadiana 20190191309 | ISBN 9781443182003 (softcover) | ISBN
9781443175999 (hardcover)
Classification: LCC PZ7.1.B85 Ano 2020 | DDC j823/.92—dc23

First published by Scholastic Australia in 2018.
This edition published by Scholastic Canada Ltd. in 2020.
Text copyright © 2018 by Laura Bunting.
Illustrations copyright © 2018 by Philip Bunting.

6 5 4 3 2 1   Printed in China CP171   20 21 22 23 24

Another book about bears.

LAURA + PHILIP BUNTING

Scholastic Canada Ltd.
Toronto New York London Auckland Sydney
Mexico City New Delhi Hong Kong Buenos Aires

Once upon a time, in a deep, dark forest, far, far away, there lived an old brown bear.

One day, the bear embarked
upon a magical

...enchanted and
behold th... ...ious Esquilax.

Before h... ...he brown bear
had wan... ...he woods
where th... ...face with
the hand... ...ale.

The... ...ppeared
to be... the... ...f the rare,
a horse with... ...f a rabbit,
and the body... ...it.

Err, bear, you're kind of interrupting my story. What's the problem?

Do you know how many books have been written about us? I'll tell you . . . too many!

Whenever you open up a book about a bear, we have to perform the story for you . . .

Even if we were in the middle of something really good — like sleeping, snoozing or napping — we have to jump up and do whatever the book says.

Why do you like reading about bears so much?

We're not so great.

We're often greedy . . .

grumpy . . .

lazy . . .

and a bit ferocious.

And we're exhausted! We are sick of doing all the work.

I see. But who will the children read about?

You can't quit!

Hmmm, we'll see about that.

The bear wore a pink tutu and rode a tiny bicycle . . .

Oh, I see. You'll make us look silly if we don't co-operate? Well, it won't work.

He chowed down on piping hot porridge.

Then upset a hive of honey bees.

And turned a frog into a handsome prince with a big, sloppy kiss.

The children cried and cried when their favourite character turned out to be a big, selfish meanie.

Oh, that's low. Fine, how about this . . . if I can find a better animal to star in your books, you'll leave us alone. No more books about bears.

Deal?

Okay. Deal.

Meet your new leading animal!

Um, bear, do you know
how many elephants
you can fit into
one tiny book?
Not many.
They're too big.

Okay, how about an echidna?
Hmmm, too spiky.

Kitten?
Too cute.

Crow?
Too noisy.

Star-nosed mole?

Too . . . whoa!

Flying fox?
Too batty.

Dodo?
Too extinct.

Crab?
Too pinchy.

Horse?
Neigh.

Peacock?
Too fancy.

Koala?
Too cuddly.

Earthworm?
Too boring.

Anglerfish?
Too ugly!

Kangaroo?
Too jumpy.

Salmon?
Hey, who
took the
salmon?

Cheetah?
Too fast.

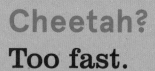

Tortoise?
Too slow.

Gazelle?
Too scaredy.

Spider?
Too scary!

Blobfish?
Seriously?

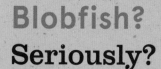

That's all I've got. They're all the animals I know.

Well, don't you see, bear? No other animal has quite what it takes to star in all those good books.

Sure, bears are a bit greedy, grumpy, lazy, and even ferocious sometimes, but who isn't?

The fact is . . . bears are just right.

So, what now?

Don't worry.
I have an idea.

Once upon a time, in a deep, dark forest, far, far away, there lived an old brown bear.

One day, the bear fell asleep and hibernated, uninterrupted, for eight long months.

Luckily, a few old friends agreed to help out while the bear took a well-deserved break.

The end.